Th

For Beth
and Amy, with love

First published 2008 by Walker Books Ltd
87 Vauxhall Walk, London SE11 5HJ

This edition published 2009

2 4 6 8 10 9 7 5 3 1

© 2008 Jan Fearnley

The right of Jan Fearnley to be identified as author/illustrator of this work has been
asserted by her in accordance with the Copyright, Designs and Patents Act 1988

This book has been typeset in Mithras

Printed in China

British Library Cataloguing in Publication Data: a catalogue record
for this book is available from the British Library

ISBN 978-1-4063-1953-8

www.walker.co.uk

WALKER BOOKS
AND SUBSIDIARIES
LONDON • BOSTON • SYDNEY • AUCKLAND

MARTHA
IN THE
MIDDLE

Jan Fearnley

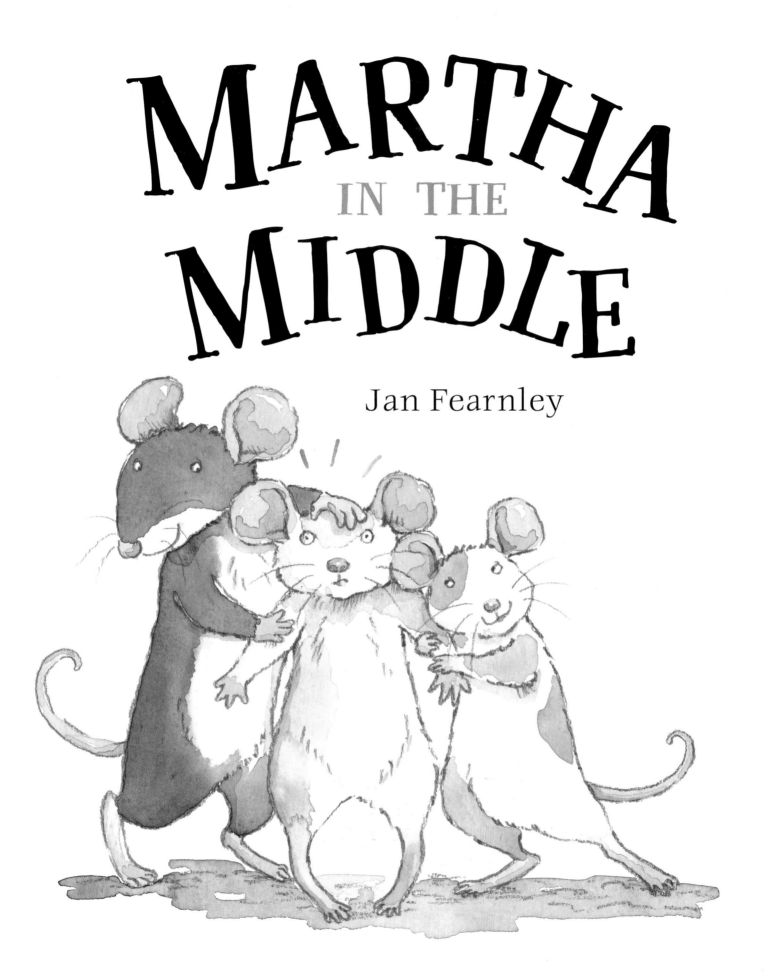

Once there were three little mice.
Clara was the eldest.

Ben was the
youngest.

And then there was Martha.

Martha was in the middle.

In fact, Martha always seemed
to be in the middle of
everything.

When they
played a game,
Martha was in
the middle.

At mealtimes,
Martha sat in the middle.

Sometimes, Martha
was squashed in
the middle,

and even when
Clara and Ben argued,
Martha was in the middle.

Clara was big and sensible.

When she did something good,
everybody said, "What a big, sensible,
grown-up girl."

I'm big and sensible
too, thought
Martha.

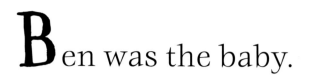

Ben was the baby.

When he did something good,
everybody said, "What a clever,
cutesy-wootsey,
little baby."

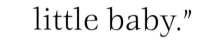

I'm cutesy-wootsey too,
thought Martha.

When Martha did something good, everybody said, "Well done, Martha."

Nobody really notices me, thought Martha.

I'm not big. I'm not the baby. I'm just me.

Sometimes she felt invisible.
Sometimes she felt very small.
Sometimes she wanted to shout,

"Here I am!"

Squashed in the middle,
invisible in the middle,

She even slept in
the middle.

One day, Martha was really fed up
with it. She decided to run
away to the bottom
of the garden.

"They won't even
notice I'm gone,"
she said.

At the end of the garden Martha met a frog.

"Hello," said the frog. "What are you doing here?"

"I've run away," said Martha, "because I hate being in the middle! The eldest is important, the youngest is the baby. But the middle doesn't matter."

The frog tutted.

"I think you're mistaken. The middle is the best bit."

"Huh!" said Martha.

The frog hopped across the lily pads.
"I'll show you some magic," he said, and he
dropped a pebble in the pool.

PLOP

Silver ripples spread from where the pebble had plopped.

"See where they come from,"
whispered the frog.

"The middle!"
said Martha.

They looked at the tall sunflowers. Martha
nibbled on some of the sunflower seeds.
"See, the seeds are in the middle,"
said the frog. "That's the
best bit."

They saw the bees buzzing round
the flowers, collecting nectar.
Each bee went right to the
centre of every
flower.

"That's the precious bit," buzzed the bees.

"Right in the middle,"
added the frog.

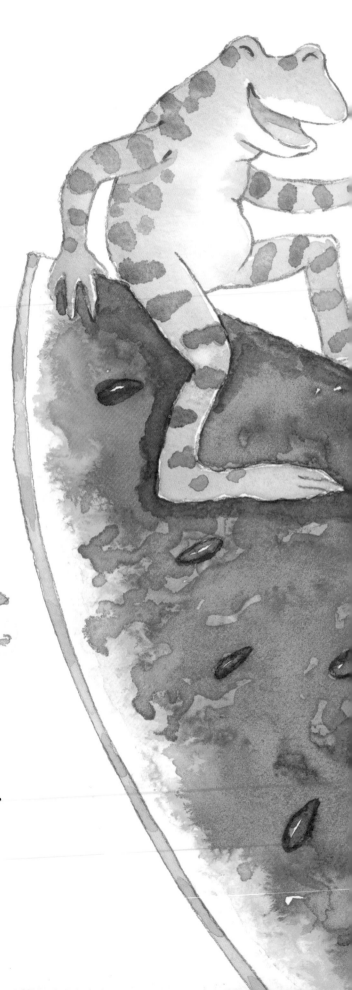

They clambered through the vegetable patch.

"Where are the sweet green peas hidden?" asked the frog. "In the middle!" said Martha.

"Where's the juiciest bit of a watermelon?" asked the frog.

"In the middle!"

shouted Martha.

"I think the middle is special,"
said Martha.

"I think you're right," smiled the frog.
"And YOU are very special indeed."

J ust then, two little faces peered
through the leaves...
It was Clara and Ben.

"Martha, have you finished
running away? We miss you."

Martha thought for a moment.
It was time to go and play.

"I think I'll run away some other day," she said.
"Goodbye!"

It didn't take long before Martha was right back in the middle of things.

And although **sometimes** she was big and sensible, and **sometimes** she was cutesy-wootsey ...

mostly she was happy
being right in the middle ...

because as any little frog
will tell you, the middle is
the **best** place
to be.

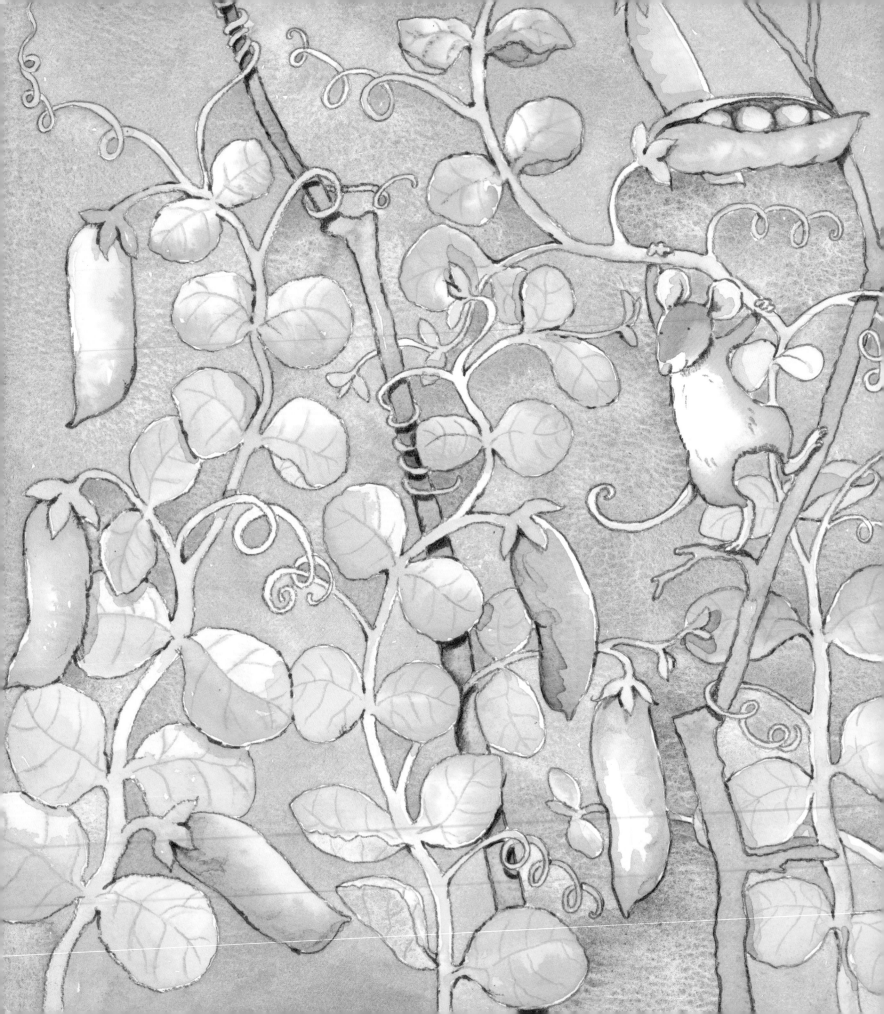

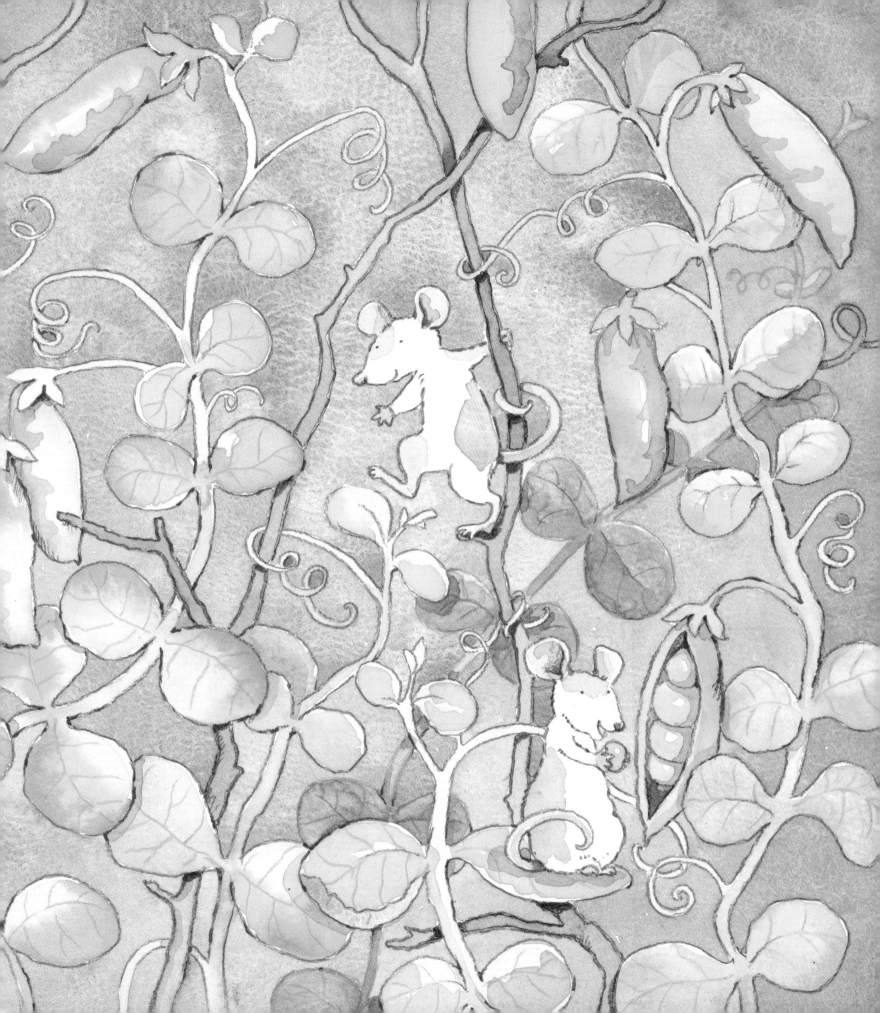

Other books by Jan Fearnley

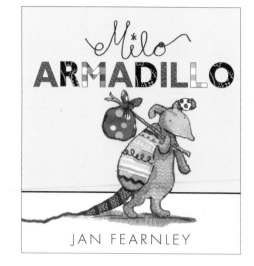

978-1-4063-1030-6

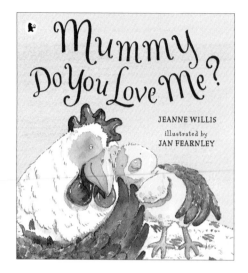

978-1-4063-1765-7

978-1-4063-0601-9

978-0-7445-9650-2

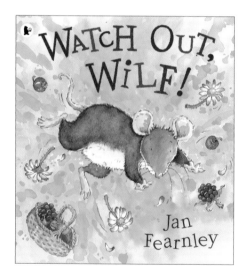

978-1-84428-509-9

Available from all good bookstores

www.walker.co.uk